THE TIGER, THE BRÂHMAN, AND THE JACKAL

A Young Owl Book  Holt, Rinehart and Winston, Inc., New York

THE TIGER, THE BRÂHMAN, AND THE JACKAL

with pictures by *MAMORU FUNAI*

From *Tales of the Punjab* by Flora Annie Steel. By
permission of The Macmillan Company, publishers.

Copyright © 1963 by Holt, Rinehart and Winston, Inc.
Library of Congress Catalog Card Number 63-12402
Printed in the United States of America

Once upon a time a tiger was caught
in a trap. He tried in vain to get out
through the bars, and rolled and bit
with rage and grief when he failed.

By chance a poor Brâhman came by.

"Let me out of this cage, O pious one!"
cried the tiger.

"Nay, my friend," replied the Brâhman mildly,
"you would probably eat me if I did."

"Not at all!" swore the tiger with many oaths.
"On the contrary, I would be forever grateful,
and serve you as a slave!"

Now when the tiger sobbed and sighed and
wept and swore, the pious Brâhman's heart
softened, and at last he consented
to open the door of the cage.

Out popped the tiger, and seizing
the poor man, cried, "What a fool you
are! What is to prevent my eating you
now, for after being cooped up so long
I am just terribly hungry!"

In vain the Brâhman pleaded for his life;
the most he could gain was a promise to abide
by the decision of the first three things
he chose to question as to the justice
of the tiger's action.

So the Brâhman first asked the *pîpal* tree what it
thought of the matter, but the *pîpal* tree replied coldly,
"What have you to complain about? Don't I give shade and shelter
to every one who passes by, and don't they in turn tear down
my branches to feed their cattle? Don't whimper—be a man!"

Then the Brâhman, sad at heart, went farther afield till he saw a buffalo turning a well-wheel; but he fared no better from it, for it answered, "You are a fool to expect gratitude! Look at me! While I gave milk they fed me on cotton-seed and oil-cake, but now I am dry, they yoke me here, and give me refuse as fodder!"

The Brâhman, still more sad, asked the road
to give him its opinion.

"My dear sir," said the road, "how foolish you are to
expect anything else! Here am I, useful to everybody,
yet all, rich and poor, great and small, trample on me
as they go past, giving me nothing but the ashes of
their pipes, and the husks of their grains!"

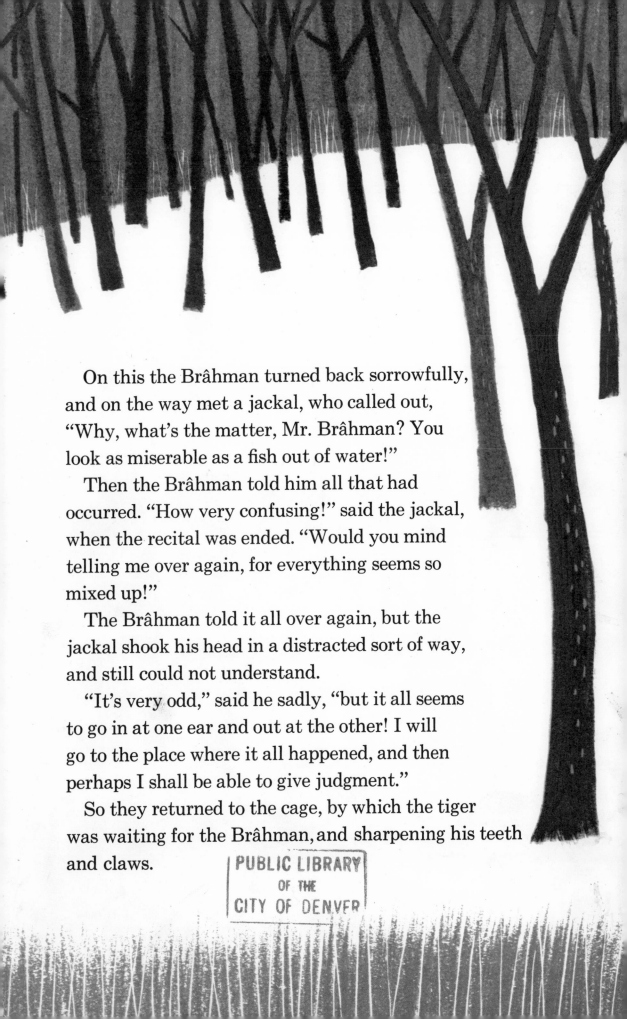

On this the Brâhman turned back sorrowfully, and on the way met a jackal, who called out, "Why, what's the matter, Mr. Brâhman? You look as miserable as a fish out of water!"

Then the Brâhman told him all that had occurred. "How very confusing!" said the jackal, when the recital was ended. "Would you mind telling me over again, for everything seems so mixed up!"

The Brâhman told it all over again, but the jackal shook his head in a distracted sort of way, and still could not understand.

"It's very odd," said he sadly, "but it all seems to go in at one ear and out at the other! I will go to the place where it all happened, and then perhaps I shall be able to give judgment."

So they returned to the cage, by which the tiger was waiting for the Brâhman, and sharpening his teeth and claws.

"You've been away a long time!"
growled the savage beast, "but now
let us begin our dinner."

"Our dinner!" thought the wretched
Brâhman, as his knees knocked together
with fright. "What a remarkably
delicate way of putting it!"

"Give me five minutes, my lord!"
he pleaded, "in order that I may
explain matters to the jackal here,
who is somewhat slow in his wits."

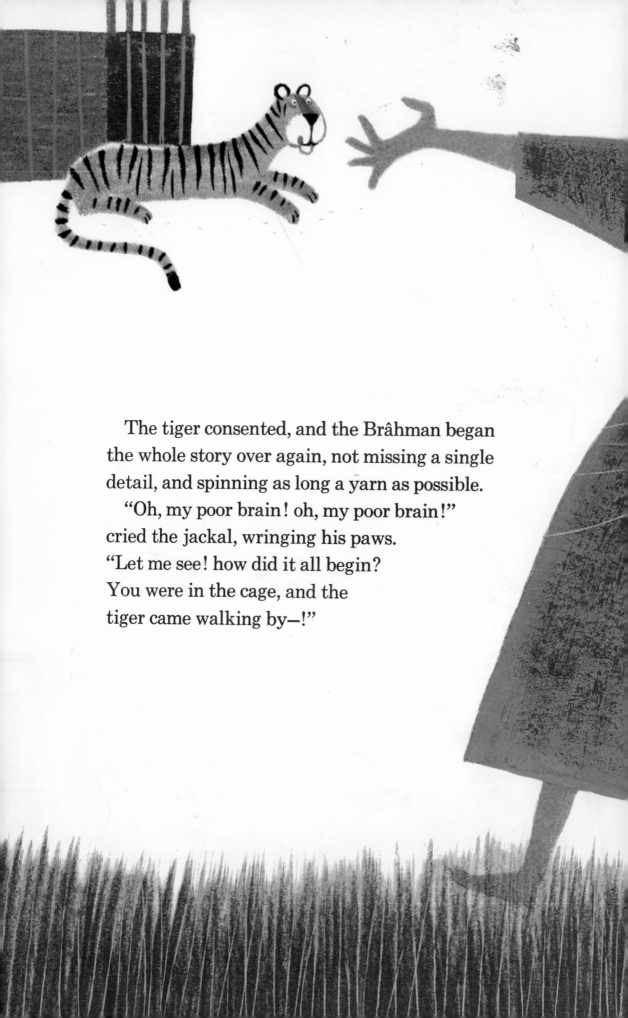

The tiger consented, and the Brâhman began
the whole story over again, not missing a single
detail, and spinning as long a yarn as possible.

"Oh, my poor brain! oh, my poor brain!"
cried the jackal, wringing his paws.
"Let me see! how did it all begin?
You were in the cage, and the
tiger came walking by—!"

"Pooh!" interrupted the tiger, "what a fool you are! *I* was in the cage."

"Of course!" cried the jackal, pretending to tremble with fright. "Yes! I was in the cage—no, I wasn't— dear! dear! where are my wits? Let me see—the tiger was in the Brâhman, and the cage came walking by—no, that's not it either! Well, don't mind me, but begin your dinner, for I shall never understand!"

"Yes, you shall!" returned the tiger,
in a rage at the jackal's stupidity.
"I'll make you understand! Look here—
I am the tiger—"

"Yes, my lord!"

"And that is the Brâhman—"

"Yes, my lord!"

"And that is the cage—"

"Yes, my lord!"

"And I was in the cage—do you understand?"

"Yes,—no— Please, my lord—"

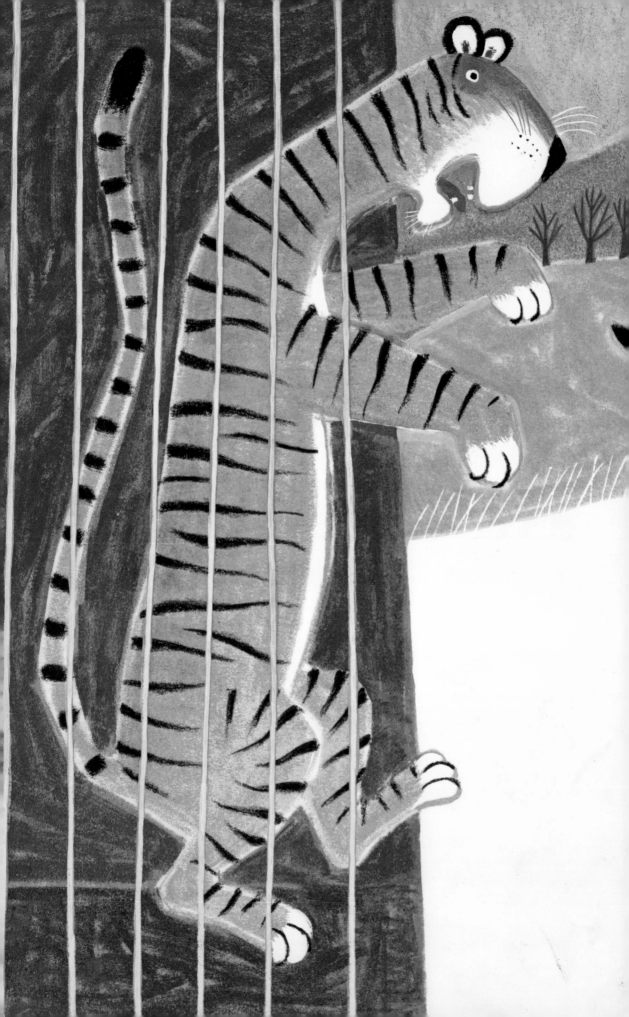

"Well?" cried the tiger, impatiently.

"Please, my lord!— how did you get in?"

"How!—why in the usual way, of course!"

"Oh dear me!—my head is beginning to whirl again! Please don't be angry, my lord, but what is the usual way?"

At this the tiger lost patience, and, jumping into the cage, cried, "This way! Now do you understand how it was?"

"Perfectly!" grinned the jackal, as he dexterously shut the door. "And if you will permit me to say so, I think matters will remain as they were!"